MEXICO CITY 4500
TORONTO WHO CARES
MELBOURNE 8300
Tokyo 700
LAGOS
MADRID 4700
NEW YORK ?
MOSCOW 4200
LONDON 4100
ROME 3900
STOCKHOLM 3900
CAPE TOWN VERY FAR
PARIS FAR
HELSINKI 3900
HAIFA 5800
ARCTIC CIRCLE 185

MILES

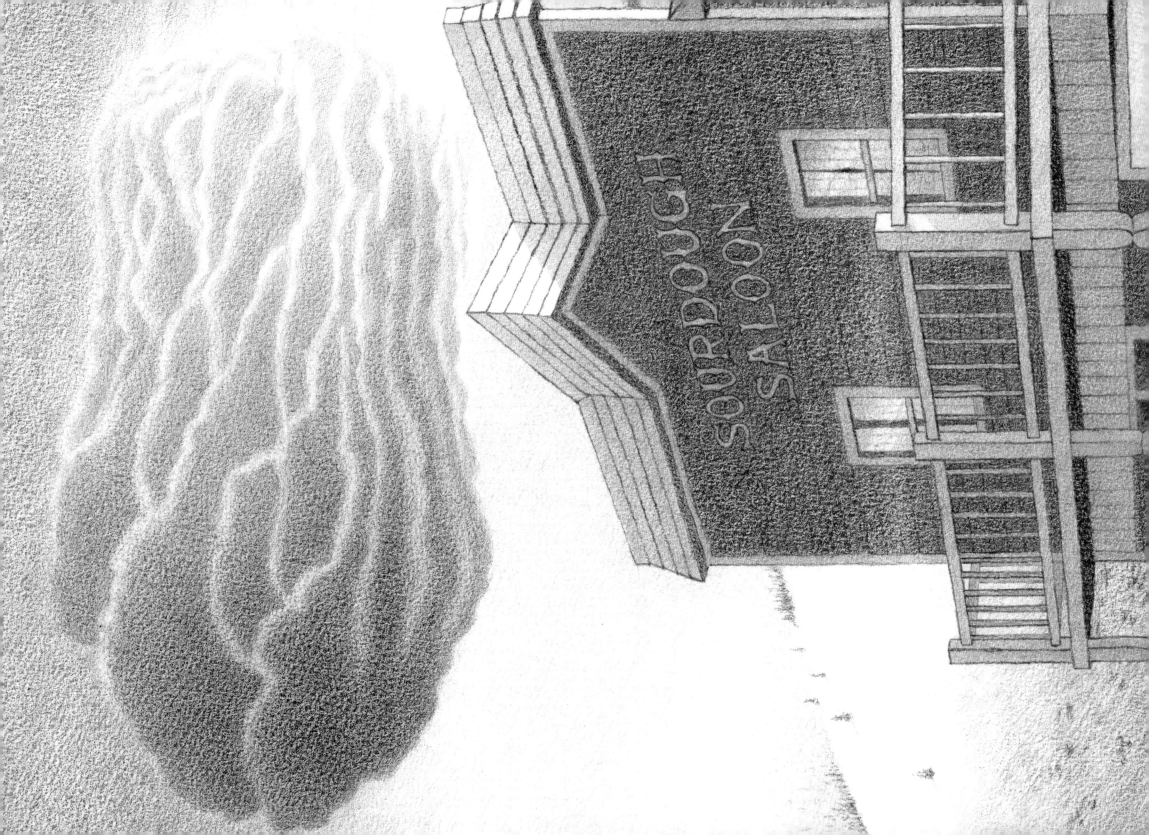

THE TRUE STORY OF
TRAPPER JACK'S
LEFT BIG TOE

IAN WALLACE

A GROUNDWOOD BOOK
DOUGLAS & McINTYRE
TORONTO AND VANCOUVER

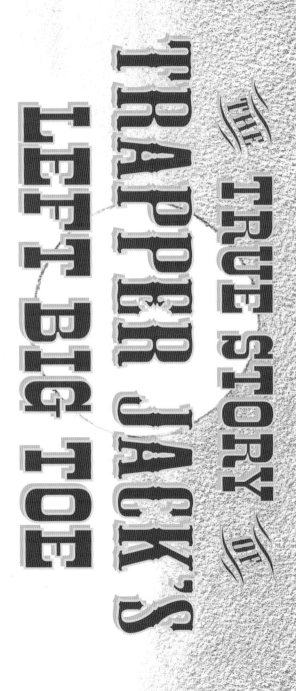

National Library of Canada Cataloguing in Publication Data
Wallace, Ian, 1950-
The true story of Trapper Jack's left big toe
A Groundwood book.
ISBN 0-88899-415-X
I. Title.
PS8595.A566T78 2001   jC813'.54   C00-932095-4

Groundwood Books / Douglas & McIntyre
720 Bathurst Street, Suite 500
Toronto, Ontario M5S 2R4

Book design by Annemarie Redmond
Printed in Hong Kong

This one is for Dawson, Joel, and Howard—and to Florence, who got me back on track

Mom and I'd been living in Dawson City for only a week when Gabe and I became friends. He introduced me to the Yukon and its mystery by telling the wildest stories that I'd ever heard. Some of them I believed. Others were pure baloney.

On our way to school one morning he stopped me cold in my tracks. "The old guy living there is Trapper Jack. He's only got nine toes. The tenth, his left big one, is inside an empty tobacco tin behind the bar at the Sourdough Saloon."

"Get off."

Gabe thumped me on the arm. "My mom's seen it."

"No way!"

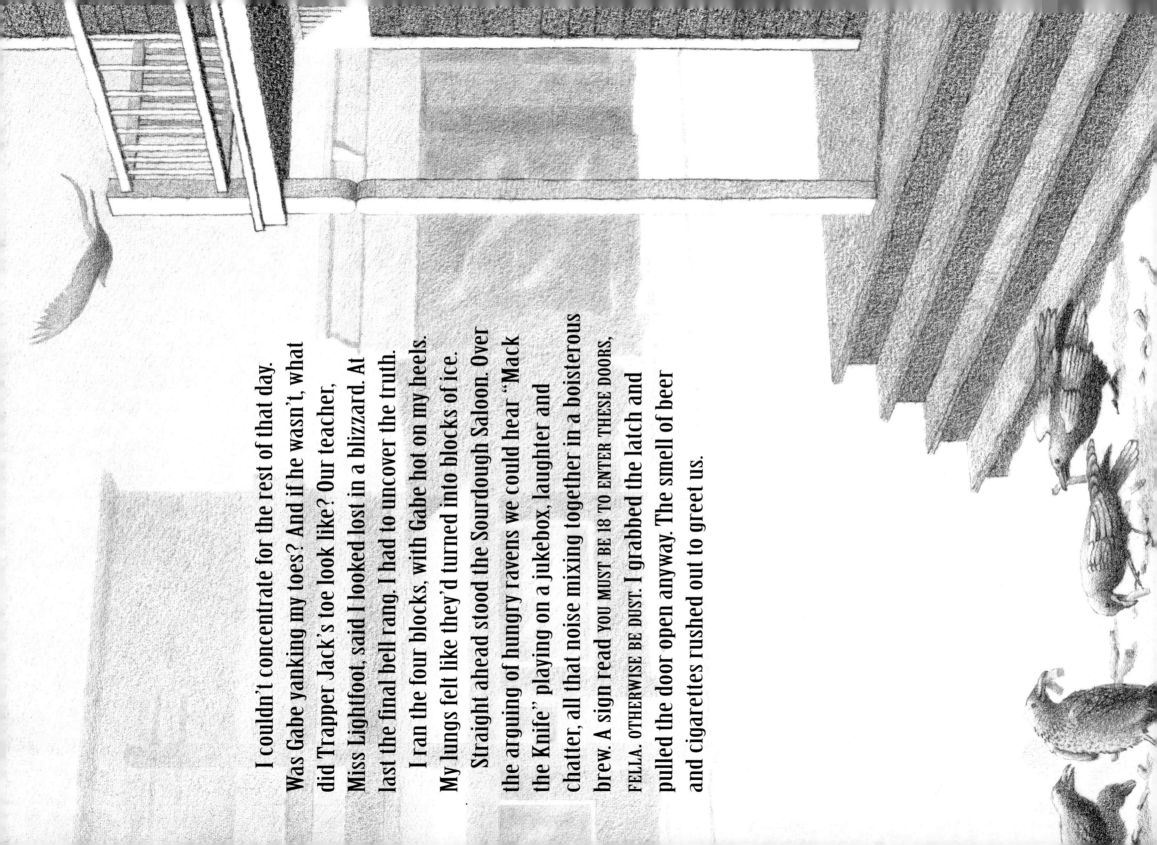

I couldn't concentrate for the rest of that day. Was Gabe yanking my toes? And if he wasn't, what did Trapper Jack's toe look like? Our teacher, Miss Lightfoot, said I looked lost in a blizzard. At last the final bell rang. I had to uncover the truth.

I ran the four blocks, with Gabe hot on my heels. My lungs felt like they'd turned into blocks of ice.

Straight ahead stood the Sourdough Saloon. Over the arguing of hungry ravens we could hear "Mack the Knife" playing on a jukebox, laughter and chatter, all that noise mixing together in a boisterous brew. A sign read YOU MUST BE 18 TO ENTER THESE DOORS, FELLA. OTHERWISE BE DUST. I grabbed the latch and pulled the door open anyway. The smell of beer and cigarettes rushed out to greet us.

Gabe yanked on my scarf. "We can't go in there!"

"Sure we can, chicken."

He cocked his head toward the street.

There stood Mr. Ironsides, our school principal. "Can I help you, boys?" he asked.

"Uh . . . no, sir," I began. "We were just . . ." I shut the door silently.

"Uh . . . reading this sign."

"I'm pleased you're reading. But there's nothing more for you to read here. Perhaps you should try the library."

We headed for home past Trapper Jack's cabin, but he wasn't there. We could tell without knocking. From the road we could see that his sled and his dogs were gone.

"Tomorrow morning, before the Sourdough opens, we'll come back," Gabe told me. "Then you'll see I'm not yankin' your toes."

The next day was Saturday, the first of April. When we reached Trapper Jack's cabin, his huskies began to bark and yowl and jump about. My eyes focused on the weathered skull above the door.

"Arctic wolf," I heard Gabe say before the door was flung open.

"QUIET OUT THERE!" barked a voice as rough as rock. Then Trapper Jack appeared in his long red underwear and his gray wool socks. He tossed some bones to his dogs. They lunged forward in a frenzy.

"Hey, Jack! It's me, Gabe Kidder. Nell's son. My mom's working on your truck. And this here is Josh. We came to see how you are."

"Warm as spit 'n just outta bed," he said. "But you'd best come inside."

We sat in the warmth of the fire while he fixed his breakfast on a wood stove. I noticed that he walked with a limp.

Finally the coffee was brewed. Three eggs were fried and smothered with Tabasco sauce, and two thick legs were pulled from the fridge. He put in his false teeth, then plunked himself in a chair. "Somethin' on yer mind, boys?"

I looked at his feet warming on a bearskin rug. "Gabe told me the wildest story about you. He said you've got only nine toes."

Trapper Jack laughed so loud and so hard that he just about choked on his teeth and his eggs. "Is that it?" he rasped and yanked off his left sock. "Frostbite. A decade ago me 'n my dogs got caught in a blindin' snowstorm out on my trapline. We fell through a soft spot in the ice." He wiggled the four remaining toes. "Two o' my dogs 'n one o' my toes didn't make it home."

"Holy cow!" Gabe grimaced.

The space where the big one should've been looked so painful I felt my own toes cringe.

"Where's your big toe now?"

Trapper Jack leaned so close that I could see he had two different-colored eyes just like his huskies. "Inside an empty tobacco tin behind the Sourdough bar."

Gabe's grin said, "I told you so."

I wanted to punch him. "Can we see it?" I blurted.

Trapper Jack stared at us for some time. "Cain't do that," he said finally. "I'm thinkin' you boys ain't got the stomach fer an amputated toe. I'm thinkin' yer bellies are as soft 'n yeller as these runny yolks." He thrust the plate toward us. The pungent smell of Tabasco sauce caught us like a right jab to the nostrils.

"Our bellies aren't soft and yellow!" I boasted. "We've seen truckloads of dead things before." Gabe squirmed in his chair. "How bad can your big toe be?"

Trapper Jack took a bite out of a duck leg. "Meet me at noon when the Sourdough opens. 'N we'll see what we'll see." By Gabe's expression, I could tell he wasn't keen on the prospect.

We went to Gabe's mom's garage to wait out the cold and the two hours. While she worked on Trapper Jack's truck, we pumped gas and I worked on Gabe, trying to convince him not to chicken out.

At noon sharp, we arrived at the Sourdough Saloon. It was real quiet except for a three-legged dog chasing its tail on the front steps.

"Hey, boy," I called out. The stray hobbled into the street, begging us to pet him.

Suddenly the door to the saloon burst open, and Trapper Jack emerged from the blackness carrying an old round tin. Gabe's hands stopped moving. He looked paralyzed.

"Prince Albert Tobacco," Trapper Jack read out loud. The sun glinted off the enamel tin, bringing a bunch of ravens swooping down from the saloon roof. Caw, caw, ya ready boys? My heart pounded in my chest. With one deft move, he lifted out something black and shriveled and held it up in front of the sun.

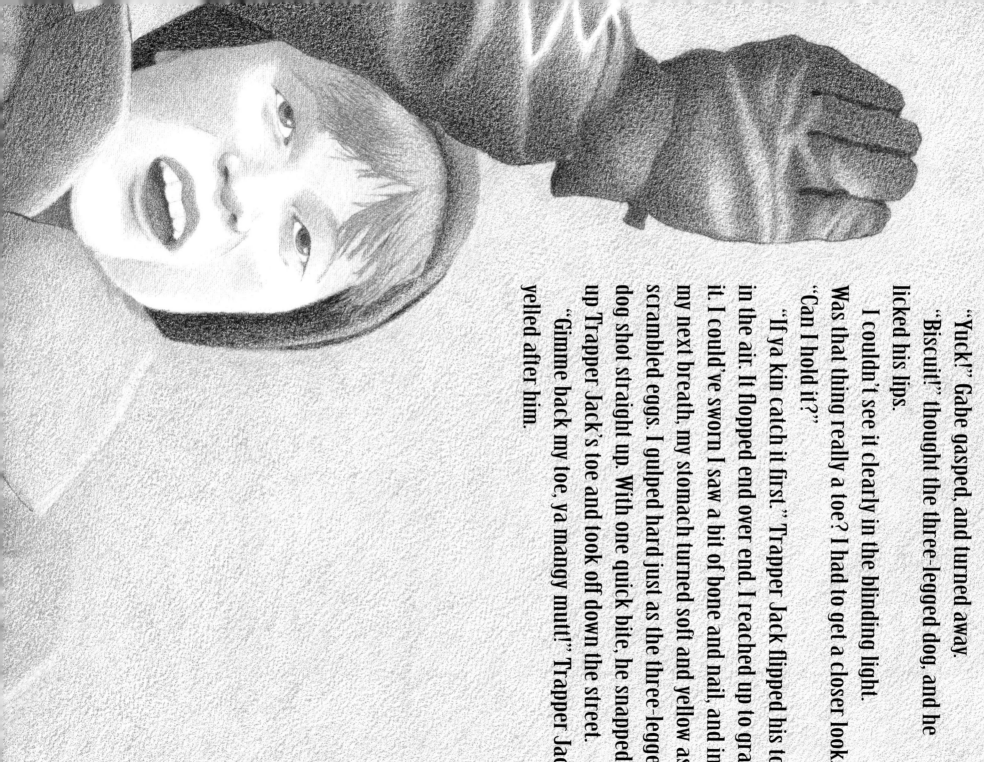

"Yuck!" Gabe gasped, and turned away.

"Biscuit!" thought the three-legged dog, and he licked his lips.

I couldn't see it clearly in the blinding light. Was that thing really a toe? I had to get a closer look. "Can I hold it?"

"If ya kin catch it first," Trapper Jack flipped his toe in the air. It flopped end over end. I reached up to grab it I could've sworn I saw a bit of bone and nail, and in my next breath, my stomach turned soft and yellow as scrambled eggs. I gulped hard just as the three-legged dog shot straight up. With one quick bite, he snapped up Trapper Jack's toe and took off down the street.

"Gimme back my toe, ya mangy mutt!" Trapper Jack yelled after him.

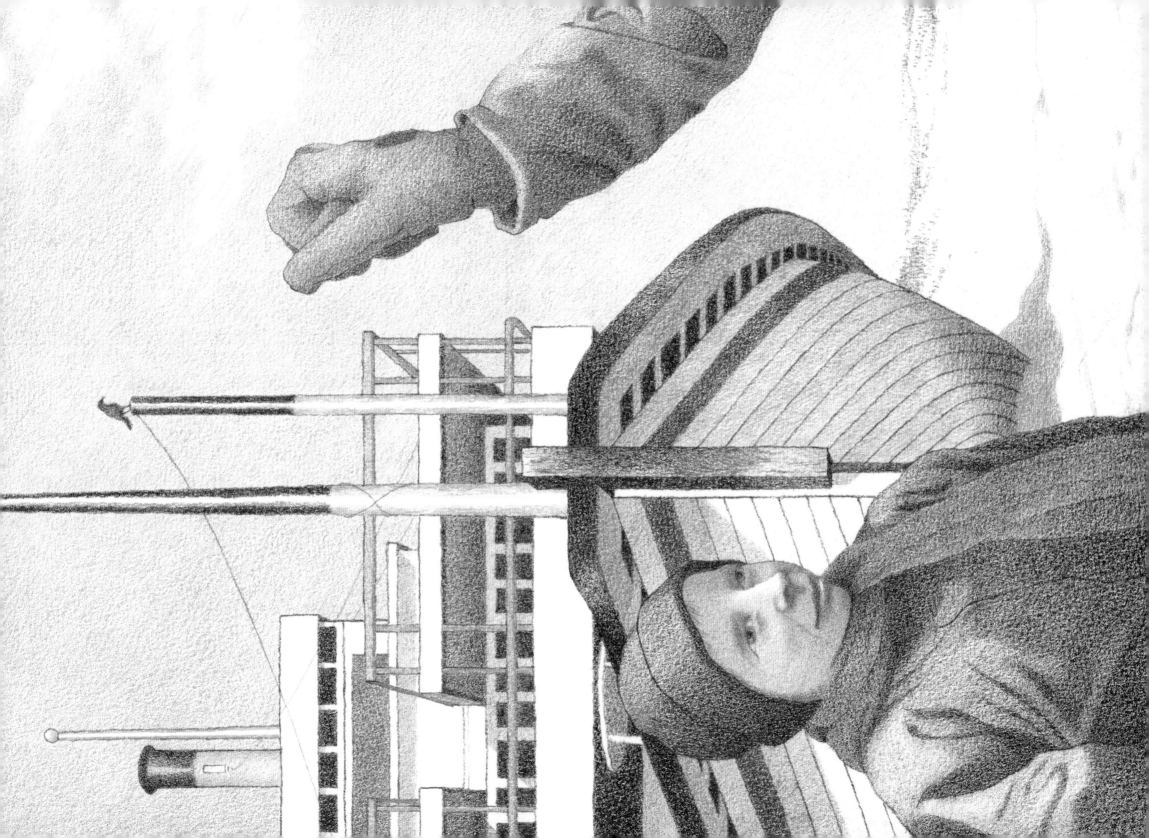

That three-legged dog was faster than the rest of us. He bounded over fences and darted around buildings with the ravens hounding his tail. When we reached the river, the icy air caught Trapper Jack, Gabe, and me hard in the lungs and brought us to a halt.

"DANG," coughed Trapper Jack, punching at the sky with both arms. "Dang, dang, bloody dog dang."

Now I knew Gabe hadn't been yanking my toes. No man in his right mind would chase a three-legged dog and a bunch of crazy ravens after a hunk of beef jerky. "I'm sorry. It's all my fault," I said.

"Ain't so, boy. This ol' fool shouldn't've flipped his toe in the air with a mangy stray 'round." Trapper Jack took a handkerchief from his pocket and blew his nose.

"Why didn't you bury it ten years ago?" Gabe asked.

"A shovel wouldn't make a dent on a bear's butt in January. When they finally cut 'er off, I stored 'er at the Sourdough. By the time summer come, I liked the idea of my toe surrounded by toe-tappin' music 'n laughter. That saloon's a much more invitin' restin' place than frozen dirt."

Gabe and I just stood there, not knowing what to say. But I thought he was right about the saloon and the dirt—and the bear.

Trapper Jack looked around the town and the surrounding hills. "This place is as wild 'n untamed as a grizzly. It kin kill a man just as quick. When I die, I'm gonna have me 'n my dogs stuffed 'n put on display at the Sourdough under a plaque that says TRAPPER JACK'S LAST STAND." He danced a little jig, kicking up snow, snorting and guffawing like a man enjoying a night at the Sourdough Saloon. "While my toe lies out in the bush somewhere. Unless that mangy three-legged dog eats it."

Gabe and I laughed at him jigging and snorting, until the three of us tumbled into a snowbank, startling a raven perched on a fence post. I stared at the bird. I couldn't believe my eyes! Something suspiciously black was squarely in its beak. And I could've sworn that I saw a bit of bone and nail.

"That scavenger's got your toe, Trapper Jack!" The raven flew silently over our heads. I charged after the bird, scooping up snow, trying to form a ball, but the snow was too dry.

"Sure thing, Josh," Gabe called out. "And I've got the other nine behind my ears. Wanna yank them, too?"

"Honest." They looked at me like I'd just told them the wildest story they'd ever heard. "It was your big toe."

"Or a prune," said Gabe.

"Or a blood sausage," said Trapper Jack, and he slid down the snowbank upside down.

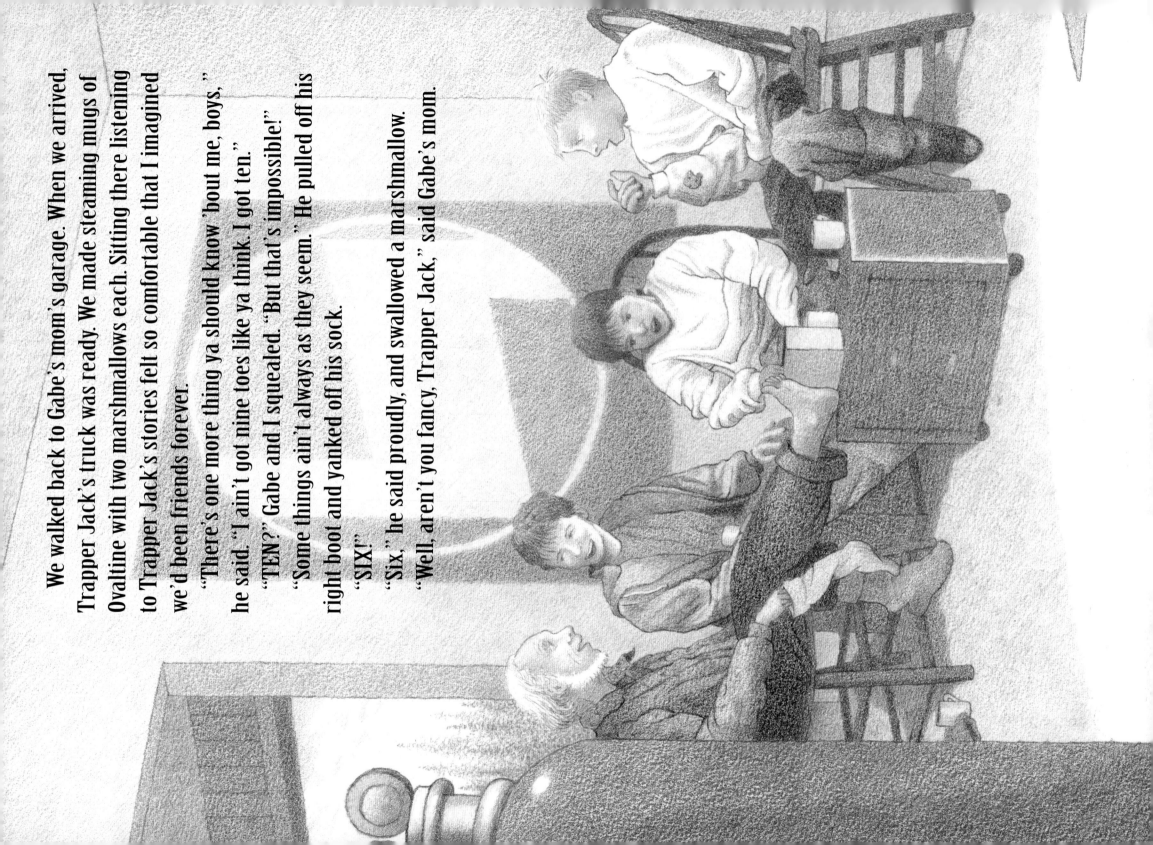

We walked back to Gabe's mom's garage. When we arrived, Trapper Jack's truck was ready. We made steaming mugs of Ovaltine with two marshmallows each. Sitting there listening to Trapper Jack's stories felt so comfortable that I imagined we'd been friends forever.

"There's one more thing ya should know 'bout me, boys," he said. "I ain't got nine toes like ya think I got ten."

"TEN?" Gabe and I squealed. "But that's impossible!"

"Some things ain't always as they seem." He pulled off his right boot and yanked off his sock.

"SIX!"

"Six," he said proudly, and swallowed a marshmallow.

"Well, aren't you fancy, Trapper Jack," said Gabe's mom.

When the Ovaltine was gone, Trapper Jack got into his truck and headed for home.

"See you next Saturday, boys," he called out.

"See you 'n yer ten toes," Gabe called back.

"That were once eleven," I threw in. Gabe's mother pulled down the garage door against the wind and the ravens as we began to howl like two three-legged dogs running loose around town.

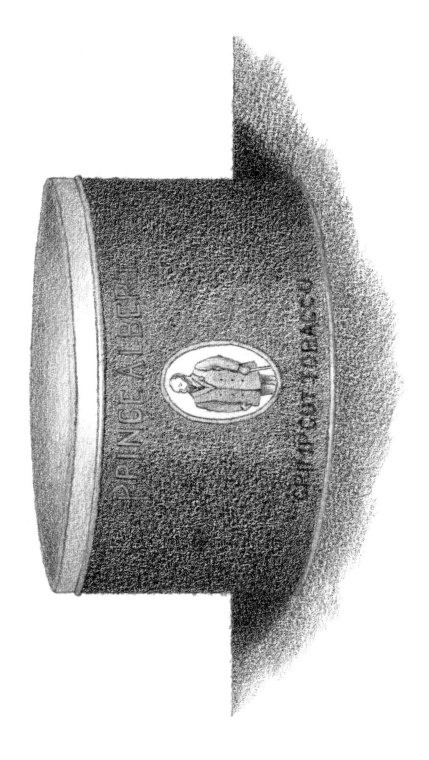

And that's Trapper Jack's story. It's all true. I wouldn't yank your toes.

Sincerely,

Joshua Yew

AUTHOR'S NOTE

You can see Trapper Jack's toe if you visit the Sourdough Saloon. And if your mom and dad are really brave, they can take part in a unique Yukon ritual, becoming members of the toughest group of people I know. People that Trapper Jack would call "Them that's kissed my toe."

All your mother (or father) has to do is order a drink from Jake, who will take Trapper Jack's toe from the Prince Albert Tobacco tin and drop it neat as an ice cube into her glass. If she tosses back the liquid, letting the toe touch her lips—then eureka, she's a member. And it's celebration time!

"Here's t' Trapper Jack 'n the mystery o' the North!"

The Sourdough's Sourtoe Cocktail Club is made up of an elite group of hardy souls whose lips have "kissed" the famous amputated toe. Jake will even give you a signed and witnessed certificate to prove what your parents did.

To date, some eighteen thousand people have embraced the spirit of the Yukon. All true. And I wouldn't yank your toes, either.

Sincerely,

Ian Wallace

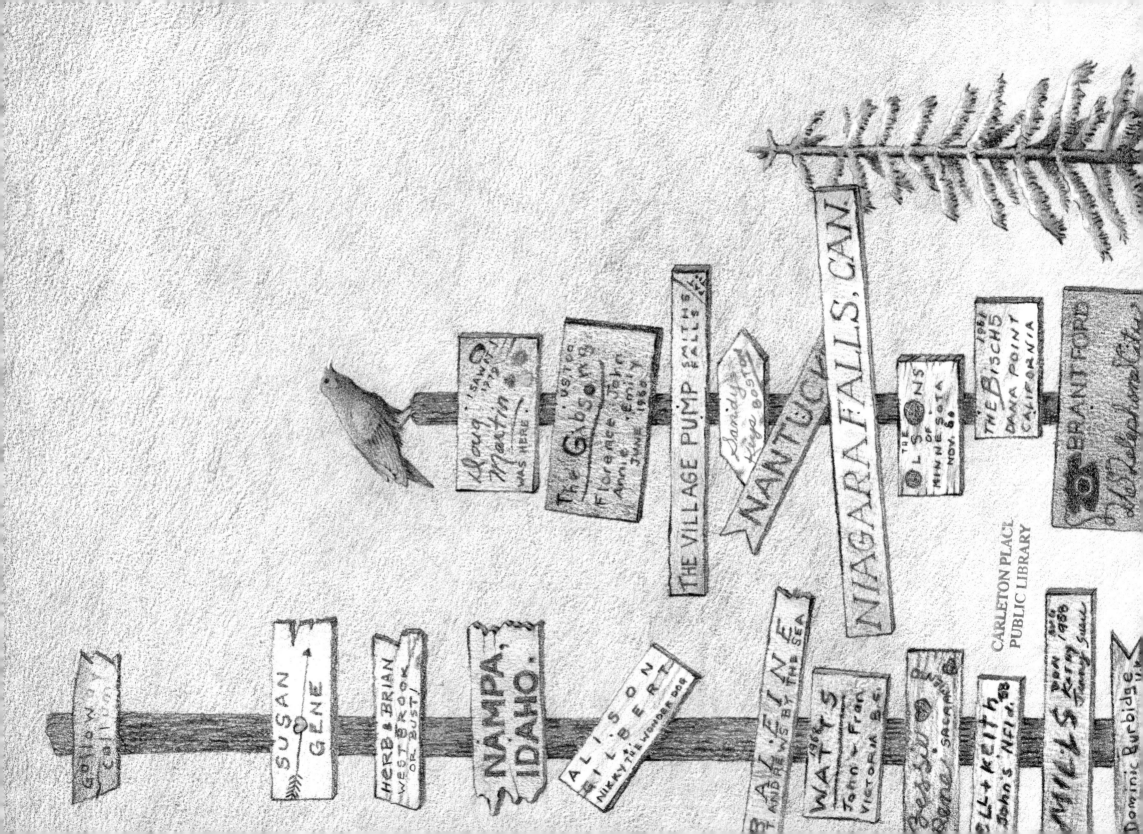